PREG-Nancy

Published by Mission Point Press
2554 Chandler Rd.
Traverse City, MI 49696
(231) 421-9513
www.MissionPointPress.com

ISBN: 978-1-965278-08-6
Library of Congress Control Number: available upon request

Printed in the United States of America

PREG-Nancy

Written & Illustrated by

Erica Gaylord

MISSION POINT PRESS

This is Nancy. Nancy loves her husband, Bob. Nancy loves to read, fish with Bob, call her mother, and drink wine with her friends.

Nancy has a great life, but there is one thing missing.

Nancy and Bob want to have a baby.

Nancy and Bob wrestle almost every other night. Sometimes, Bob ends up on top. Other times, Nancy pins Bob down.

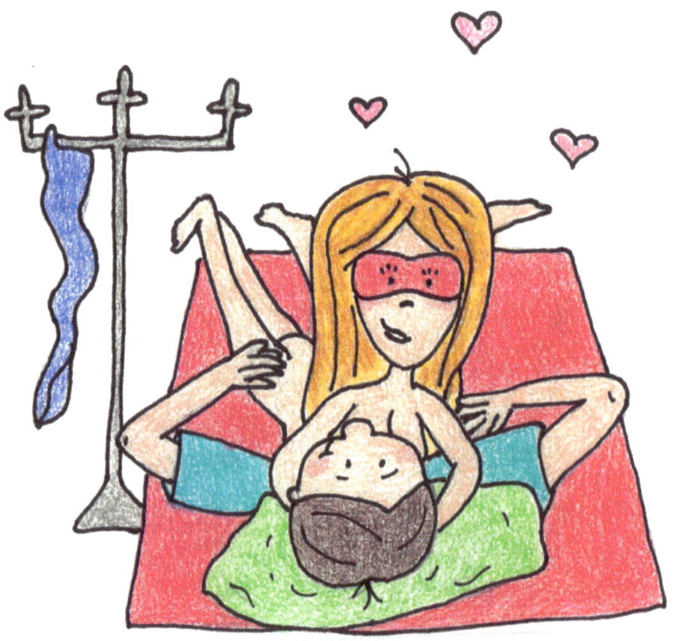

It doesn't really matter who ends up on the top or bottom. Wrestling is fun!

Even though she enjoys her regular matches with Bob, Nancy is sad. It seems like she will never get pregnant. She sees her friends getting pregnant. It is hard to feel happy for them at times.

"Something must be wrong with me," thinks Nancy. She cries herself to sleep.

Nancy wakes up one morning and just feels *different*. She decides to privately take a pregnancy test. It feels like ages for the results to appear.

She squints to see two parallel lines and cannot believe her eyes. The test is positive! Nancy has officially become *Preg-Nancy*!

Preg-Nancy calls Bob into the bathroom and shows him her positive test. Bob looks so happy, which makes Preg-Nancy start to sob.

"We should celebrate!" says Bob. "I'll get wi—sparkling grape juice!"

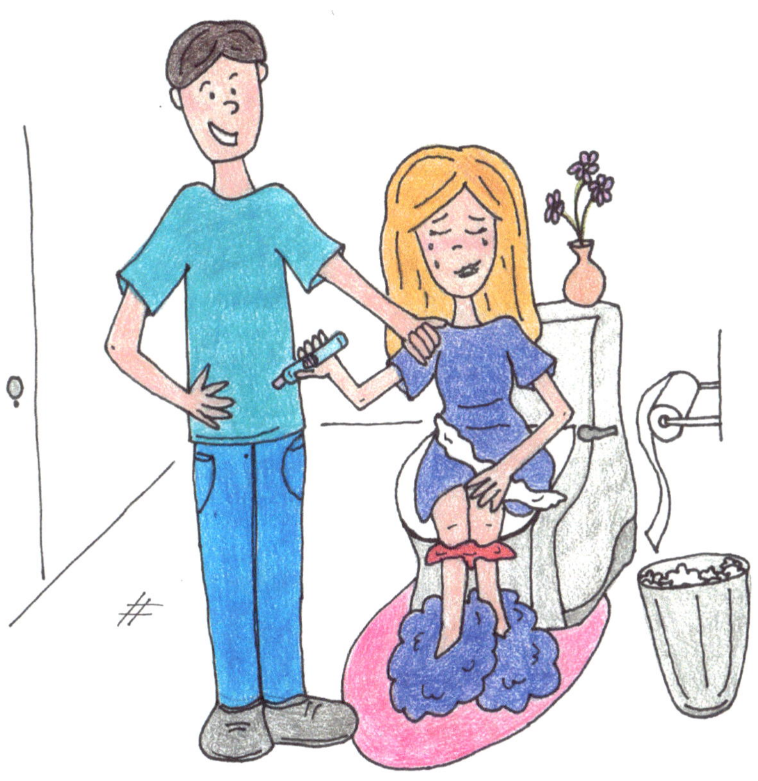

That sounds pretty good to Preg-Nancy.

The happy couple cannot wait to share the news with Preg-Nancy's mother, Barb.

An anxious week goes by and Barb stops for a visit. Preg-Nancy hands her a book titled, *How to be a Fantastic Grandma.*

"But I'm not a grandma," says Barb.

Bob gives her a wink. "You are now!" he says.

Barb bursts into tears and Preg-Nancy starts crying once more.

Preg-Nancy feels sick. *Very* sick. Preg-Nancy can hardly move without feeling the urge to vomit.

"This is worse than the time I got food poisoning at Thanksgiving!" she says to Bob.

Bob wonders how to make Preg-Nancy feel better. He rushes to the store for lots of snacks, ginger ale, and antacids.

When Bob returns home, Preg-Nancy is fast asleep on the couch. She looks so cute lying in a pool of her own drool.

Preg-Nancy expected the first ultrasound to be over her tummy. Instead, the doctor sticks a wand down *there.* Preg-Nancy is surprised, but Bob is the one who is blushing.

"It's alright, Bob. This won't take long," says the doctor.

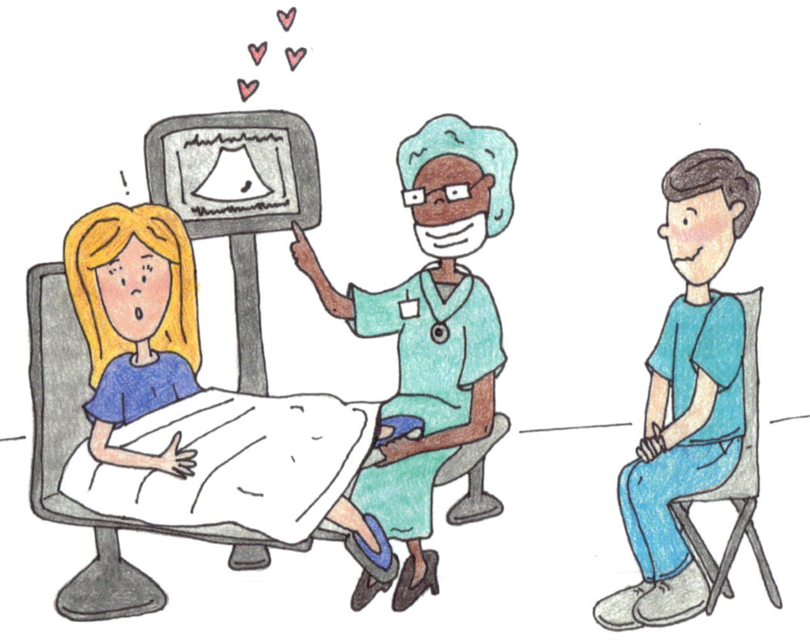

They see their tiny baby for the first time. When they hear the heart beating, Preg-Nancy starts to cry... *again.*

Even though Bob is her best friend, Preg-Nancy
sometimes feels angry with him.

"Bob, you can't do anything right!" she yells, when
Bob accidentally drops a bucket of popcorn onto the
floor.

Bob knows that Preg-Nancy doesn't mean everything
she says.

Preg-Nancy tries to remember to take her daily
vitamins and eat lots of healthy fruits and vegetables.
But it all makes her gassy. Gassier than ever.

Bob pretends not to notice.

Preg-Nancy is more watermelon-shaped by the month. Walking is a challenge and sleeping is so uncomfortable.

By far the worst inconvenience is that Preg-Nancy always needs to pee—*always*.

Preg-Nancy is jealous that Bob can fully empty his bladder anytime he wants.

"Why, I oughta!" says Preg-Nancy as Bob relieves himself over the side of their fishing boat.

Preg-Nancy feels hungrier by the minute. The doctor says she should gain a total of about 15 pounds.

Preg-Nancy has already gained 20, and she still has two months to go.

"Oh well. The baby really wants pizza," thinks Preg-Nancy. "Mmmmm...pepperoni with extra cheese," she decides.

Preg-Nancy feels the baby shifting inside her belly.

"Wow! Do you see this, Bob!?" asks Preg-Nancy.

"Missed it!" says Bob.

"Well, feel this!" says Preg-Nancy, grabbing his wrist and placing his hand where a tiny foot presses painfully against her spleen.

"I can't feel anything," says Bob.

Every time Bob tries to feel the baby, the baby stops moving.

"Maybe next time," says Preg-Nancy.

One day, Preg-Nancy does not feel the baby moving at all. She calls her doctor. At the appointment, the doctor tells her she has elevated blood pressure.

"I wonder why?" thinks Preg-Nancy after she sped 45 miles, avoided a fender bender, and ran up three flights of stairs to the Women's Clinic.

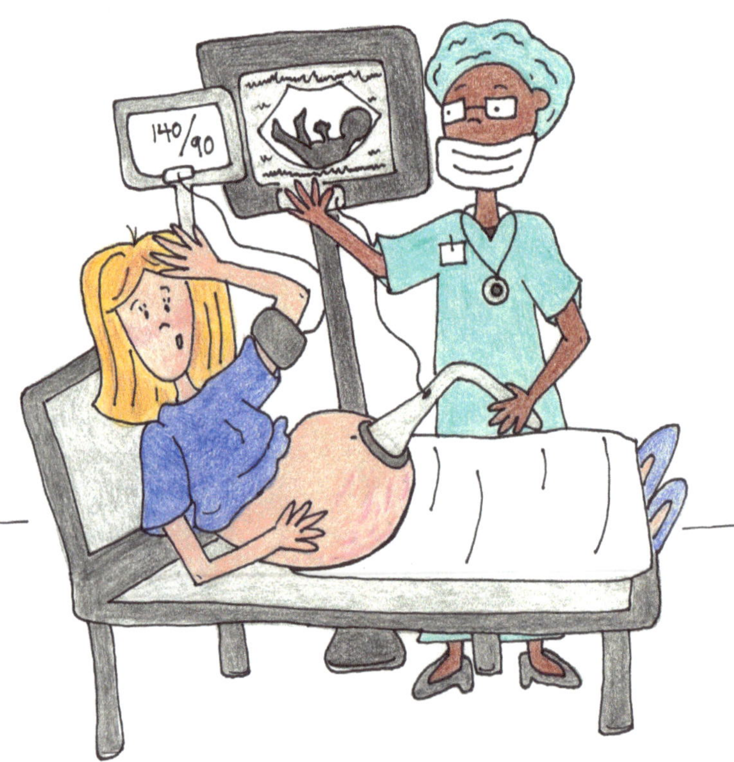

Preg-Nancy is overwhelmed, but the baby is fine.

"The baby was just asleep," says the doctor.

It is the holidays, and everyone is drinking. Preg-Nancy really wants some wine. She leans over and takes a big whiff of Barb's Cabernet Sauvignon.

"Ahhh, it's just not the same," she sighs.

Bob hands her the last piece of cherry cheesecake with homemade caramel sauce.

Cheesecake makes Preg-Nancy feel better.

Preg-Nancy greets her Baby Shower guests.

Preg-Nancy's aunt promptly pulls a measuring tape from deep within her purse and wraps it around Preg-Nancy's belly.

"Goodness! You're as round as you are tall!" her aunt exclaims.

"Oh, thank you," says Preg-Nancy.

It is almost time for the baby to come. Preg-Nancy has everything ready. Well, except the nursery should be re-organized. The baby clothes could be re-washed. The bottles could be steamed once again.

"I know! I'll pack my hospital bag!" exclaims Preg-Nancy.

"You've had it packed for weeks," says Bob.

"I mean I'll re-pack it!" counters Preg-Nancy.

"Everything will be perfect," says Bob.

Preg-Nancy feels awful. She is so tired from contractions all day.

"Stay in there, baby," says Preg-Nancy. "You can't come until your due date!"

Preg-Nancy gets up from the couch in a hurry.

"Bob, my contractions are less than five minutes apart. It has been like this for over an hour!"

Bob stares at her.

"We have to go, NOW!" yells Preg-Nancy.

Bob grabs the bags.

Bob and Preg-Nancy begin their frantic drive to the hospital.

"What if the baby is ugly?" asks Preg-Nancy as she breathes her way through contractions in the passenger seat.

"Is that what you're worried about right now?" asks Bob.

Preg-Nancy has been worried about that her entire life.

The parents-to-be finally arrive at the hospital. Bob parks in the emergency parking lot instead of dropping her off at the entrance.

Preg-Nancy walks further than she would have liked.

Preg-Nancy checks into triage feeling nervous. Less now about the possible physical appearance of her new baby...

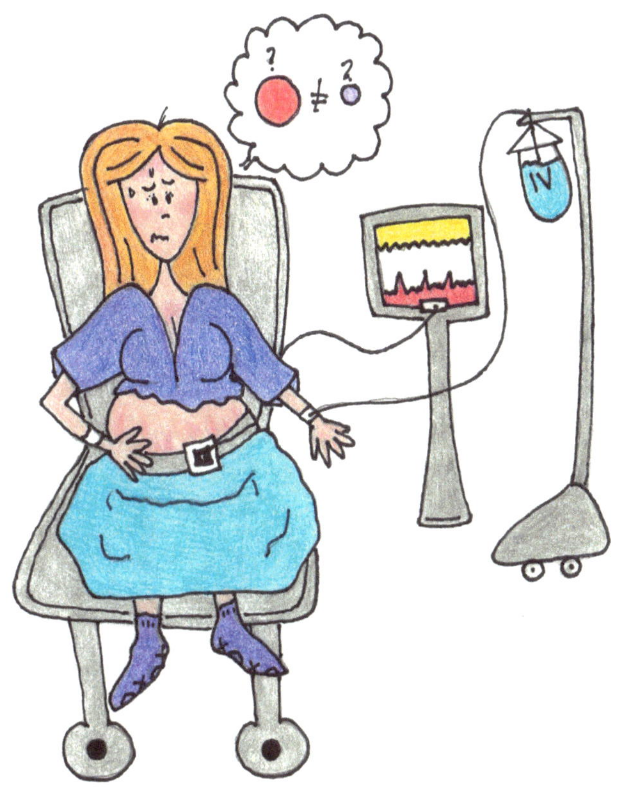

...more about the fact that she will inevitably squeeze a grapefruit out of a grape.

In their room, the nurse asks Preg-Nancy her pain level.

"Compared to what?" asks Preg-Nancy.

"Ummm...good question," says the nurse. "Would you like an epidural?"

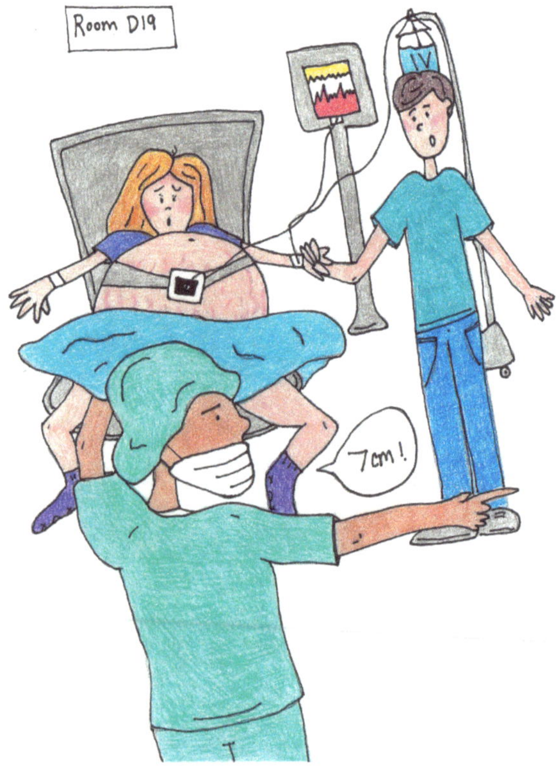

The nurse checks Preg-Nancy's dilation.

"Never mind," says the nurse. "We won't have time."

Preg-Nancy is already at seven centimeters! The nurse calls the doctor in to break her water.

Now dilated to ten centimeters, Preg-Nancy is sweating and breathing heavily. She is ready to push out the baby. There are a lot of doctors, nurses, and other medical staff in the room.

"Three, two, one—PUSH!" they tell Preg-Nancy.

They repeat this process over and over. It really hurts Preg-Nancy. The pressure feels as if her butt will explode. It is the worst pain she has ever experienced.

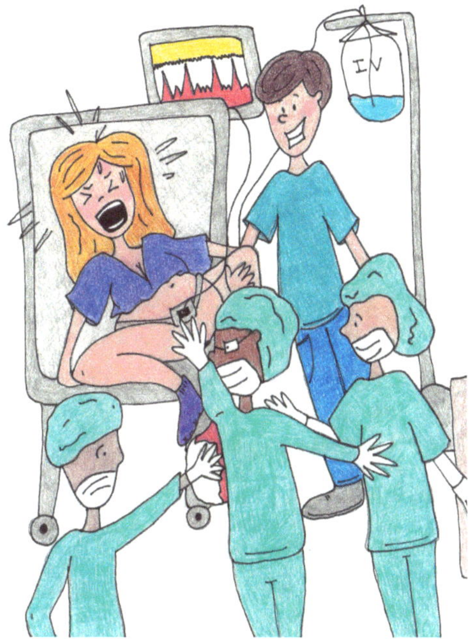

"You did this to me!" she screams at Bob.

"You're doing great! I can see the baby's head!" says Bob, grinning.

Preg-Nancy is not sure the pain will ever end.

One last push and the baby is out!

"It's a boy!" announces the doctor.

It is Bob's turn to cry. Nancy holds her baby for the first time. He is the most perfect thing in the entire world.

Nancy knows her adventure was all worth it.

Erica Gaylord, a native of Mesick, Michigan, owns Northern Lights Insurance Agency in her hometown. She graduated from Mesick Consolidated Schools in 2009 before earning her associate's degree with honors from Northwestern Michigan College. She then attended Ferris State University, where she graduated Summa Cum Laude with a bachelor's degree in Business Administration. Erica then went on to receive her Master of Business Administration Degree with a certificate in Advanced Studies in Management Tools and Concepts, achieving the highest distinction.

When she's not in her professional office setting, Erica enjoys a vibrant and fun home life with her husband and three children. She loves kid snuggles, artsy home projects, and exploring the hiking trails of Manistee National Forest. Her passions include Bluegrass music, pontoon rides, Disney World podcasts, and savoring anything her husband cooks.

Preg-Nancy is Erica's debut book.